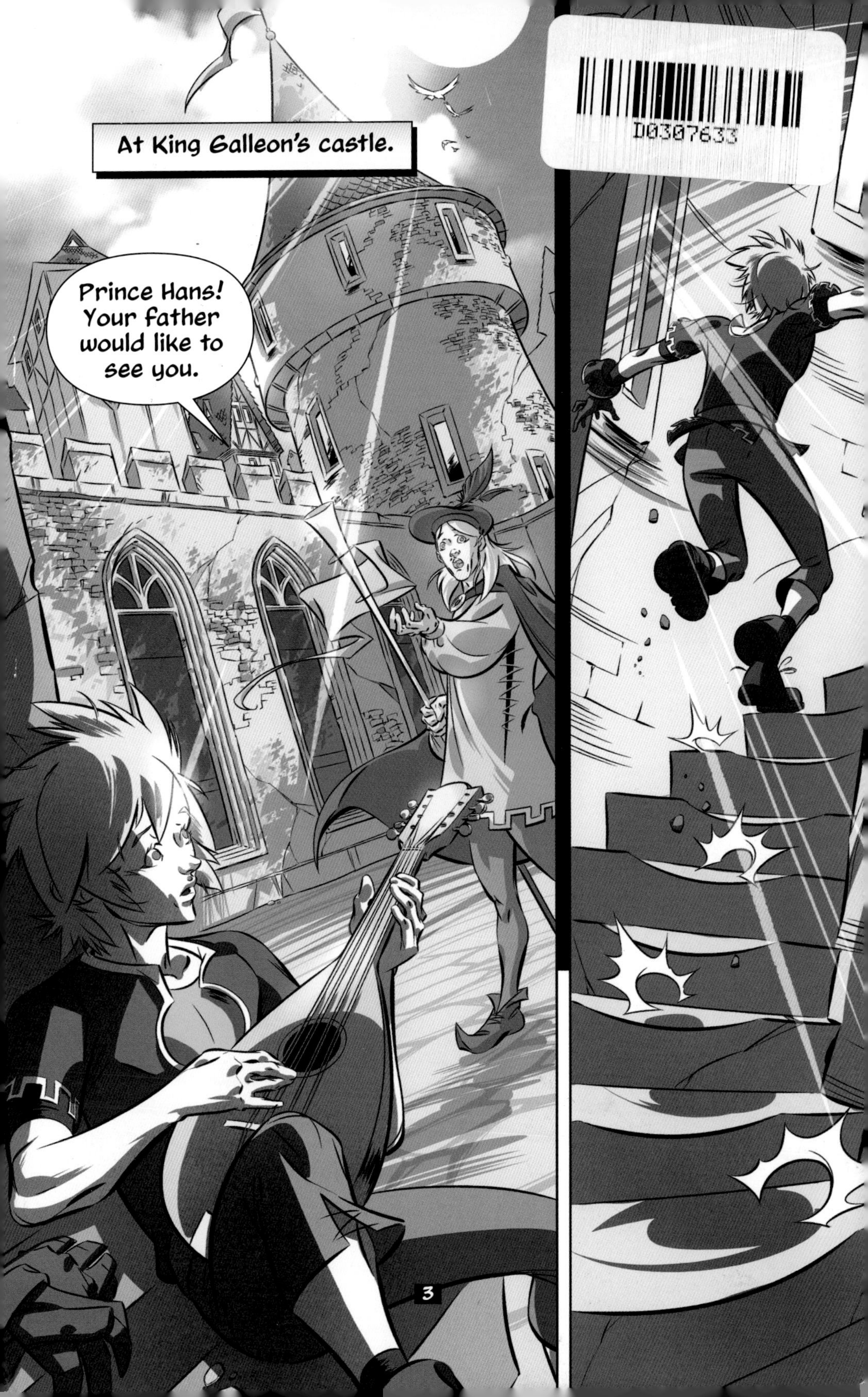
At King Galleon's castle.
Prince Hans! Your father would like to see you.

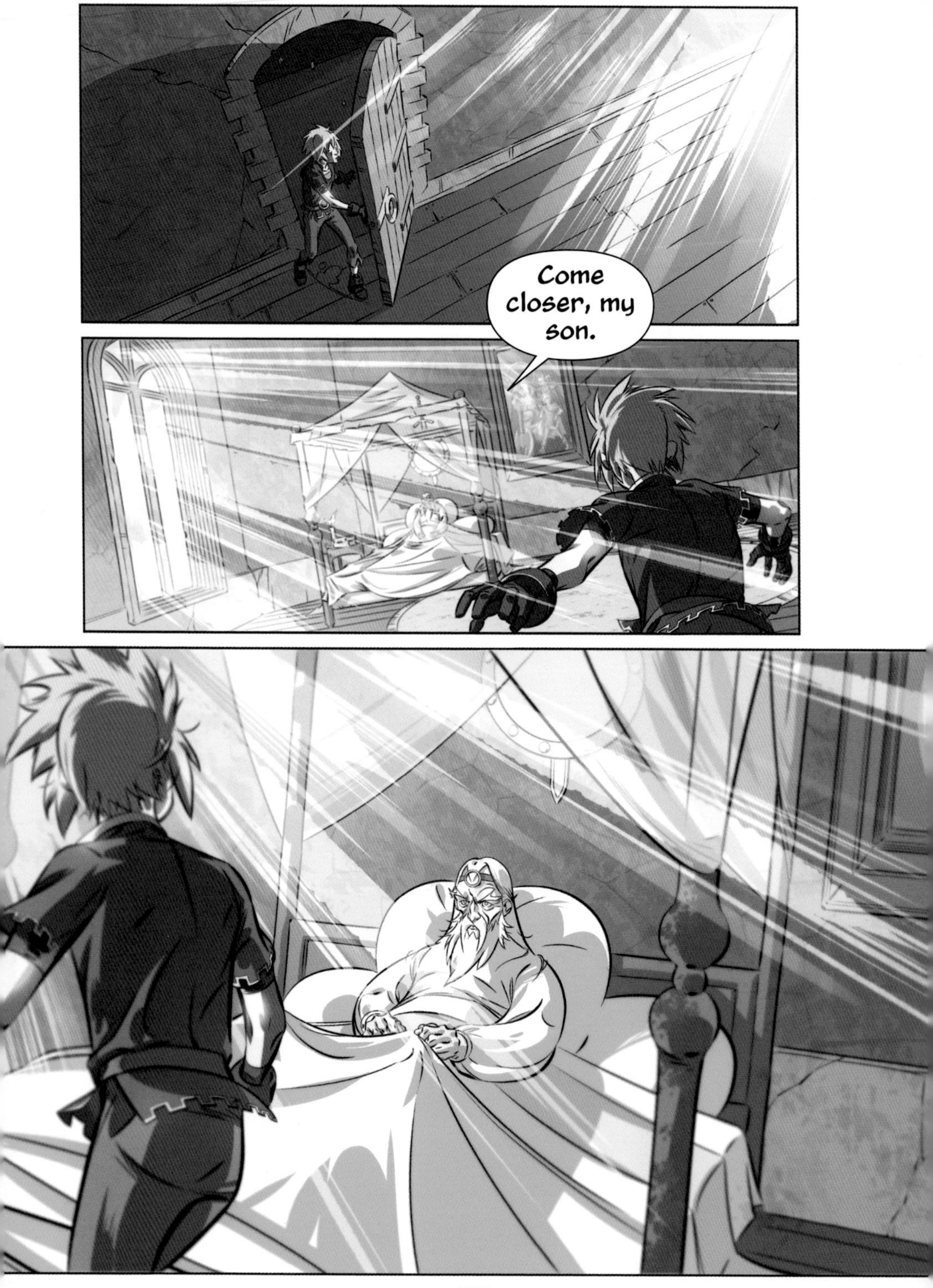
Come closer, my son.

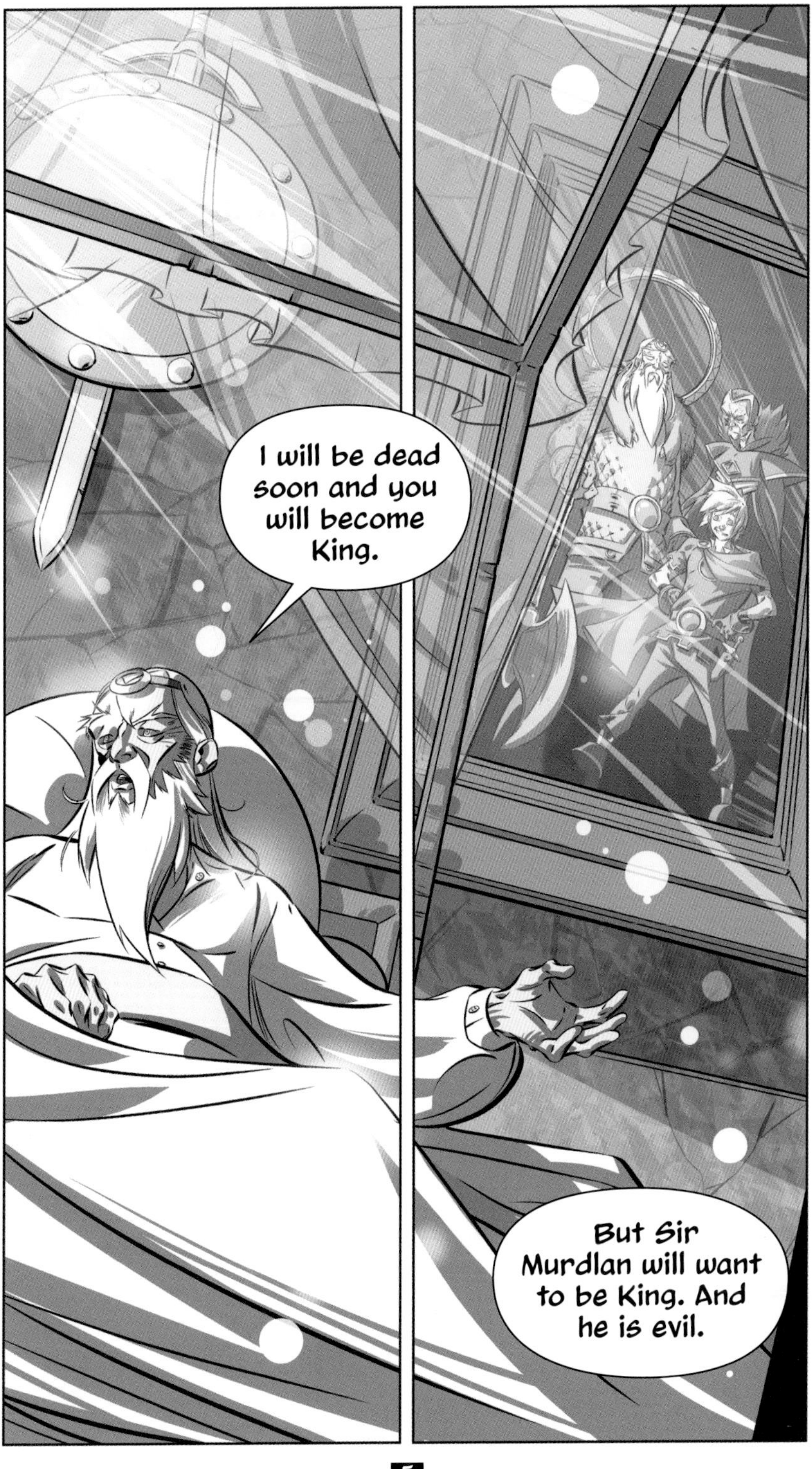
I will be dead soon and you will become King.
But Sir Murdlan will want to be King. And he is evil.

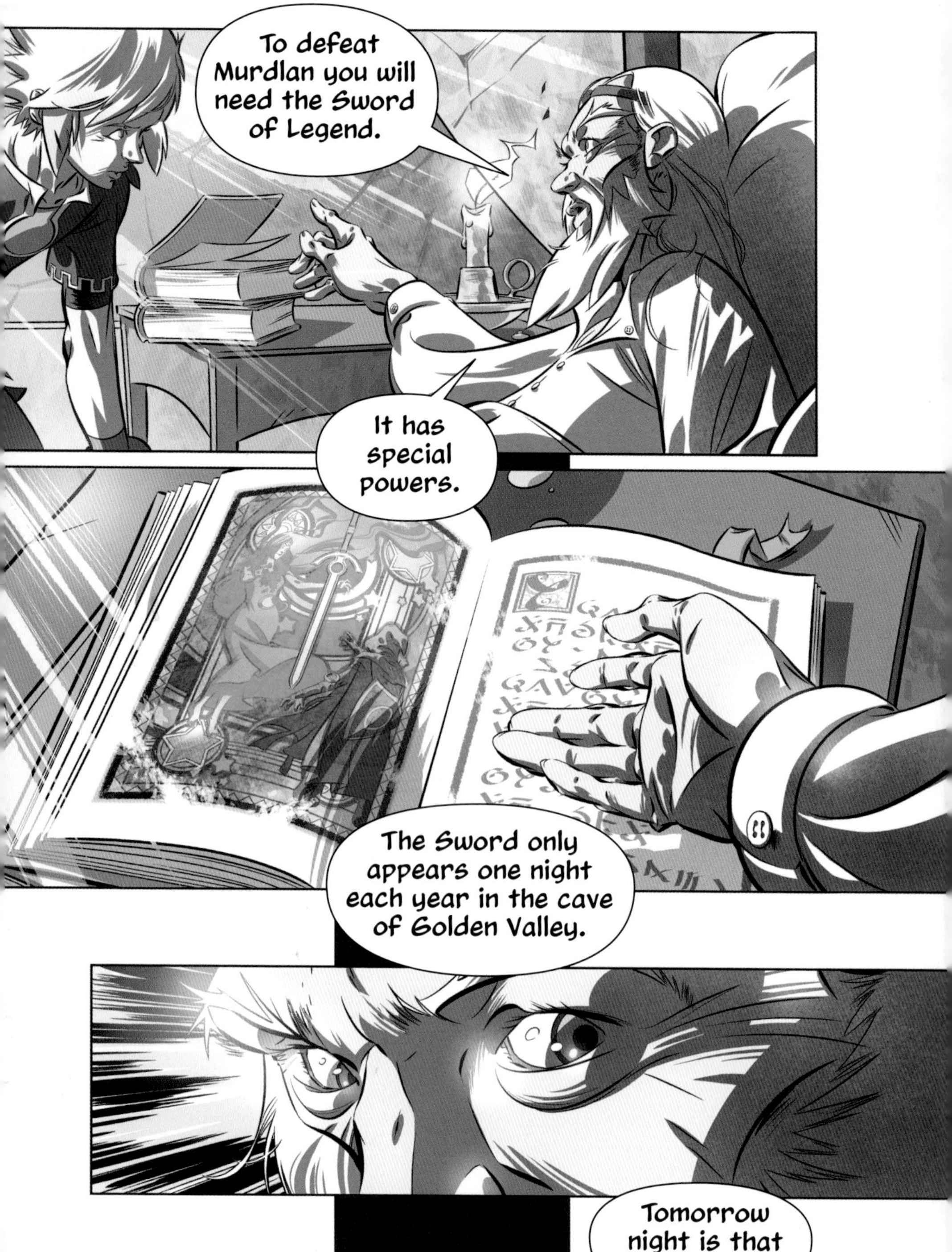
To defeat Murdlan you will need the Sword of Legend.
It has special powers.
The Sword only appears one night each year in the cave of Golden Valley.
Tomorrow night is that night.

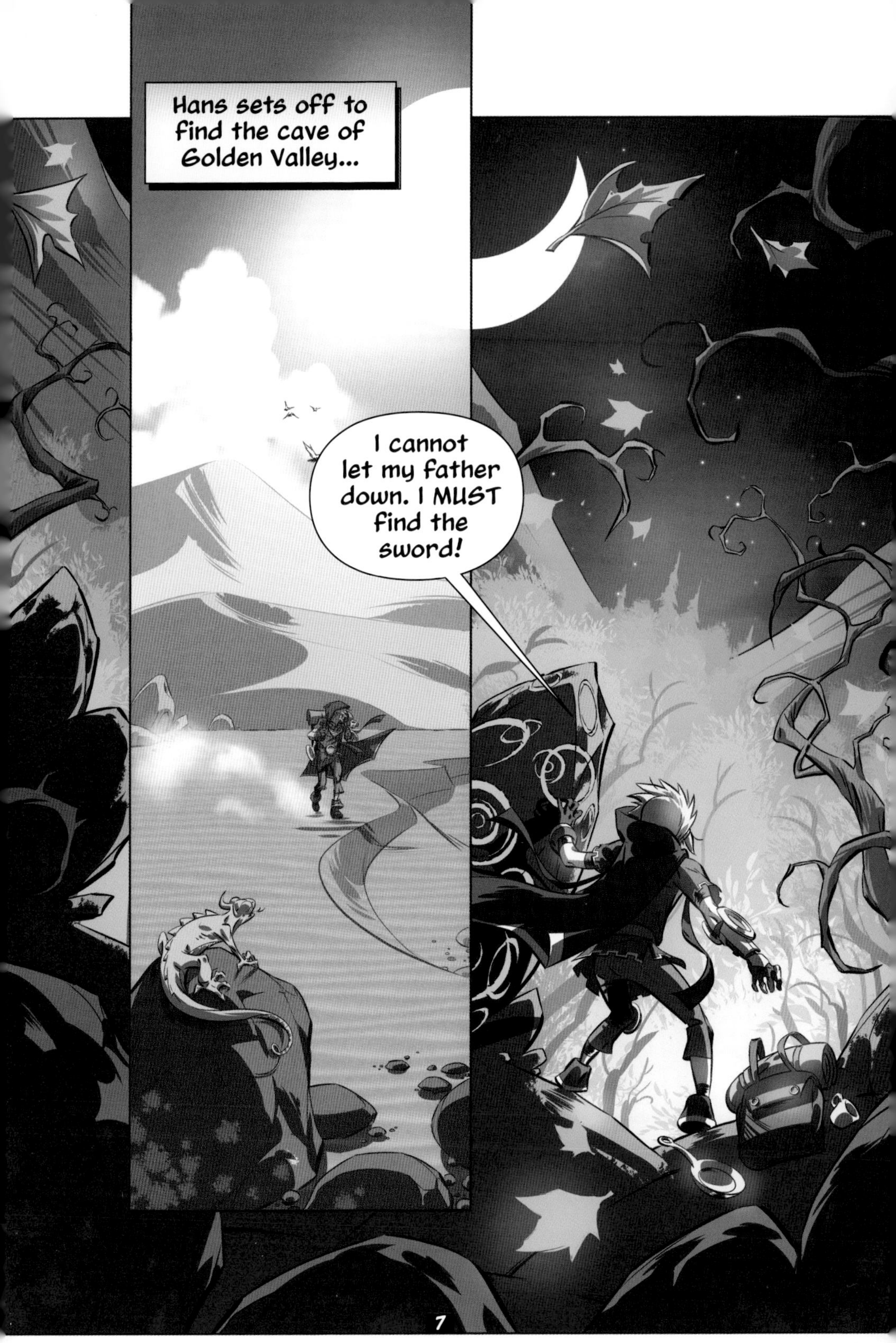
Hans sets off to find the cave of Golden Valley...
I cannot let my father down. I MUST find the sword!

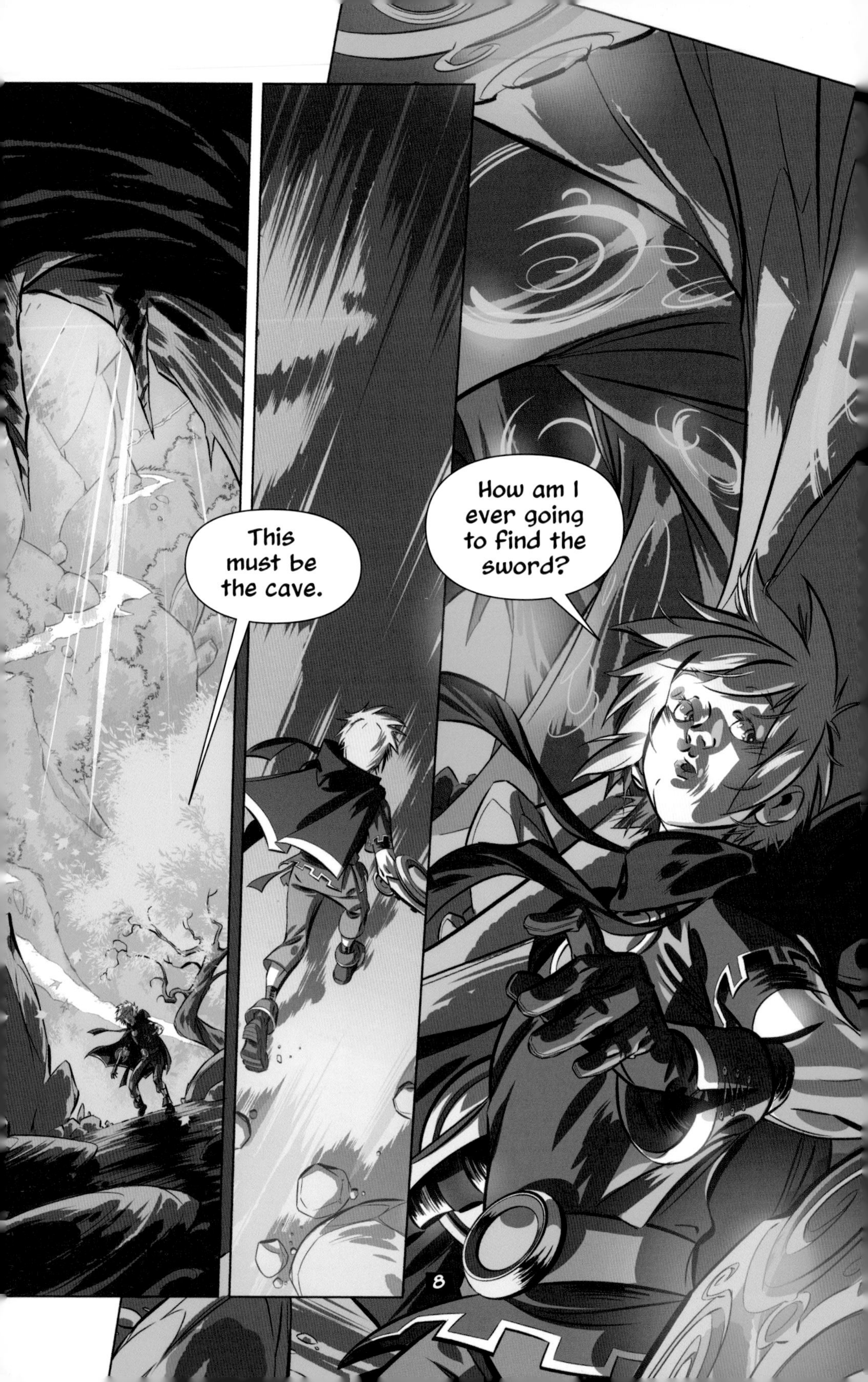
This must be the cave.
How am I ever going to find the sword?

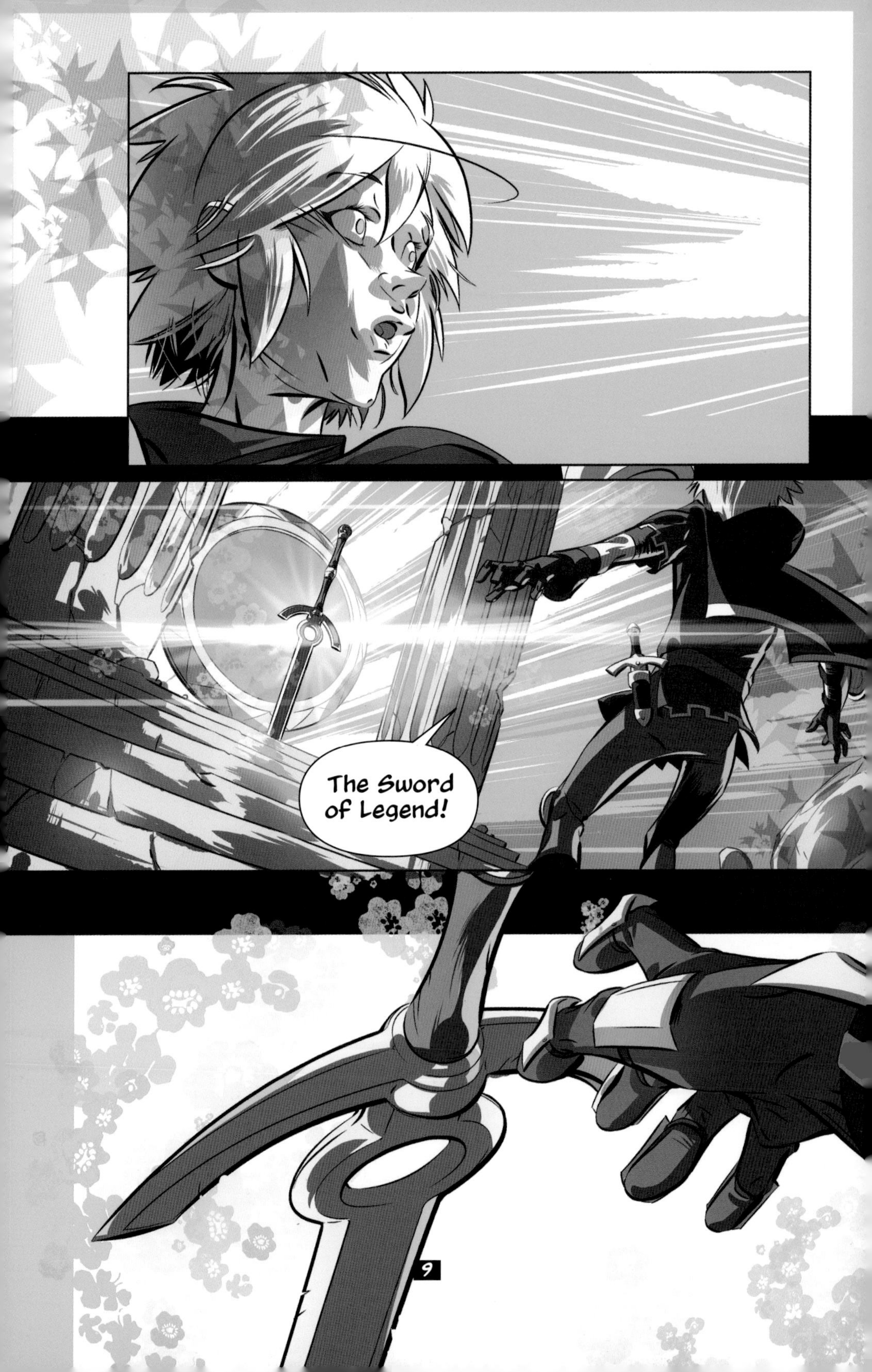
The Sword of Legend!

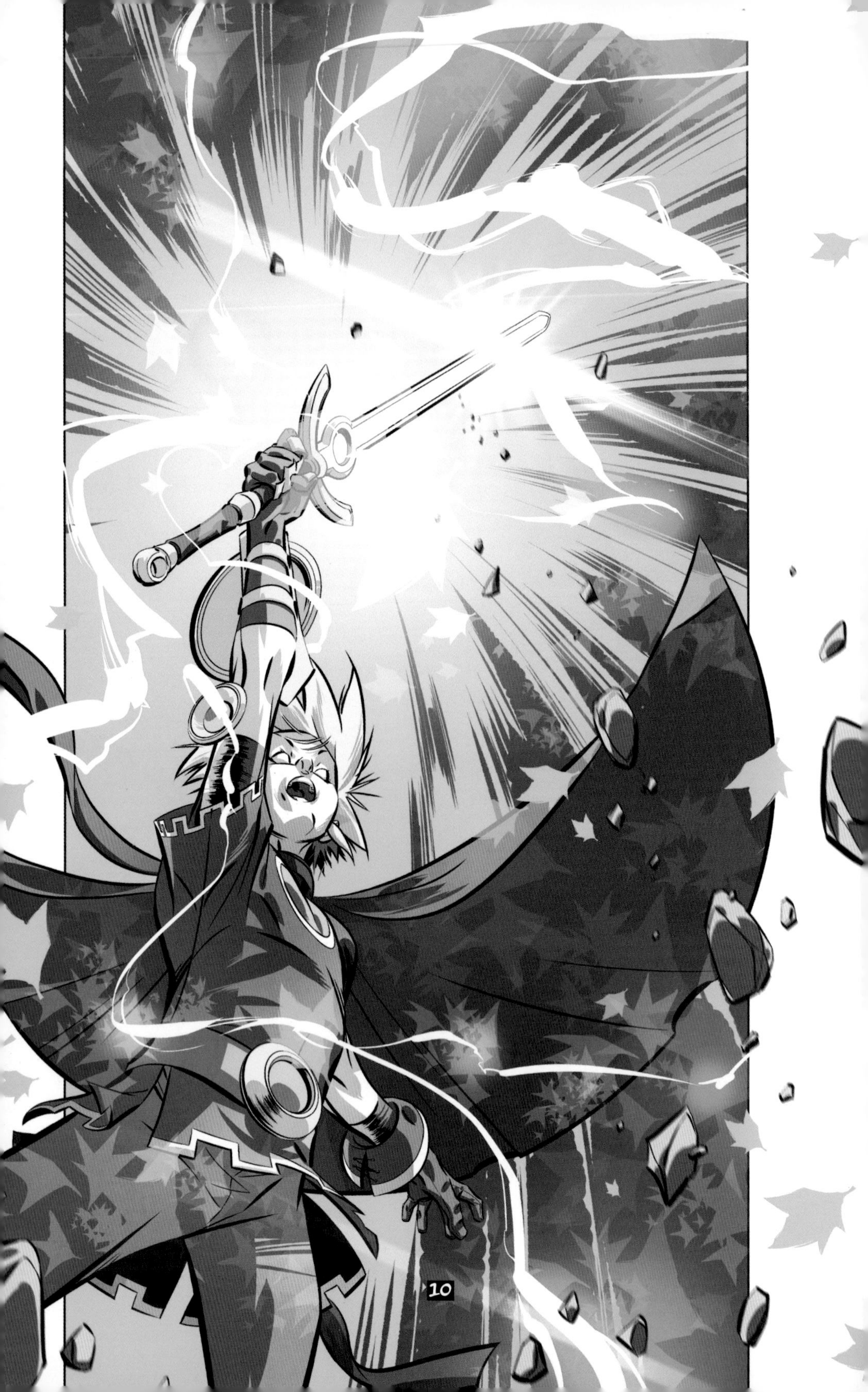

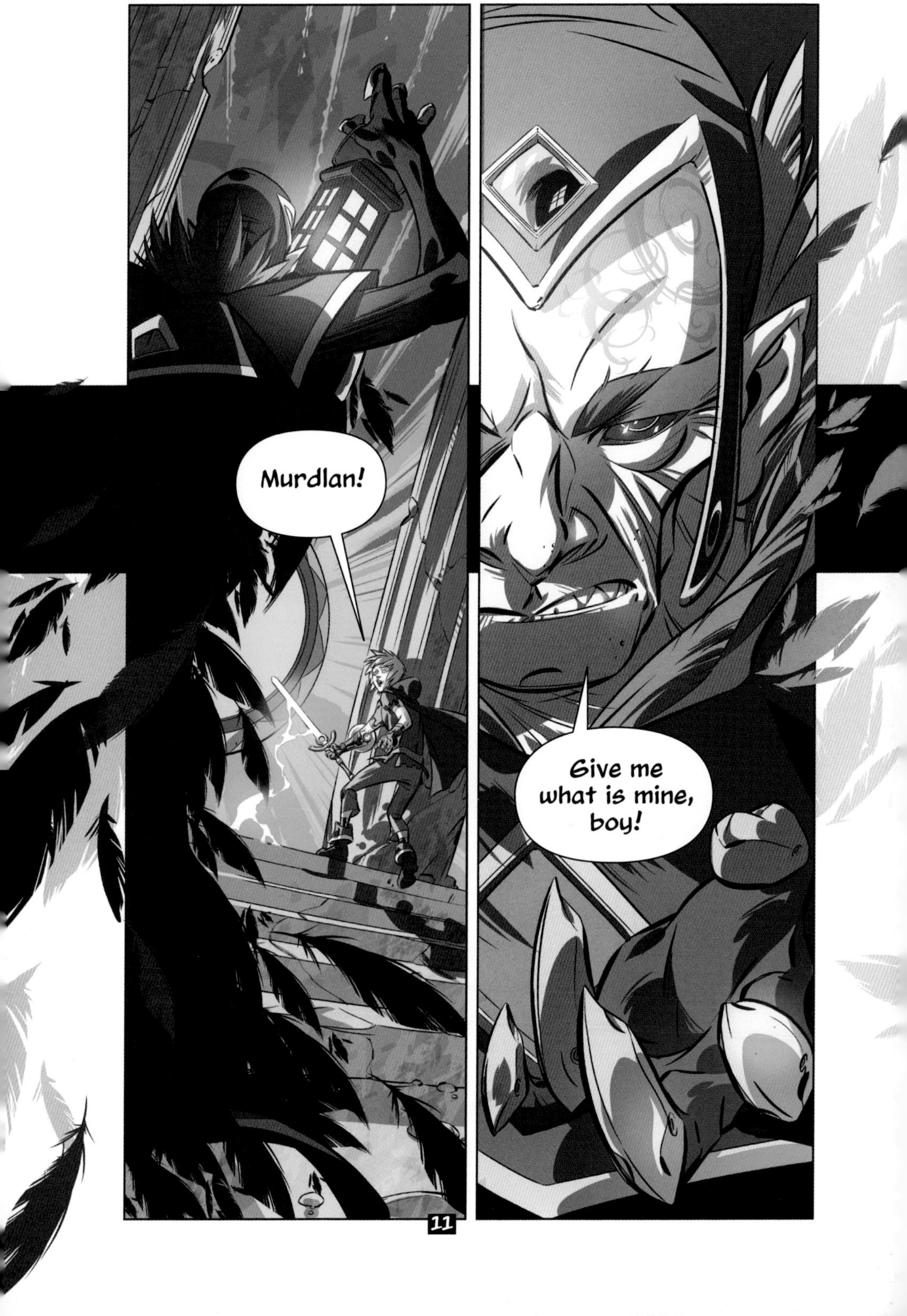
Murdlan!
Give me what is mine, boy!

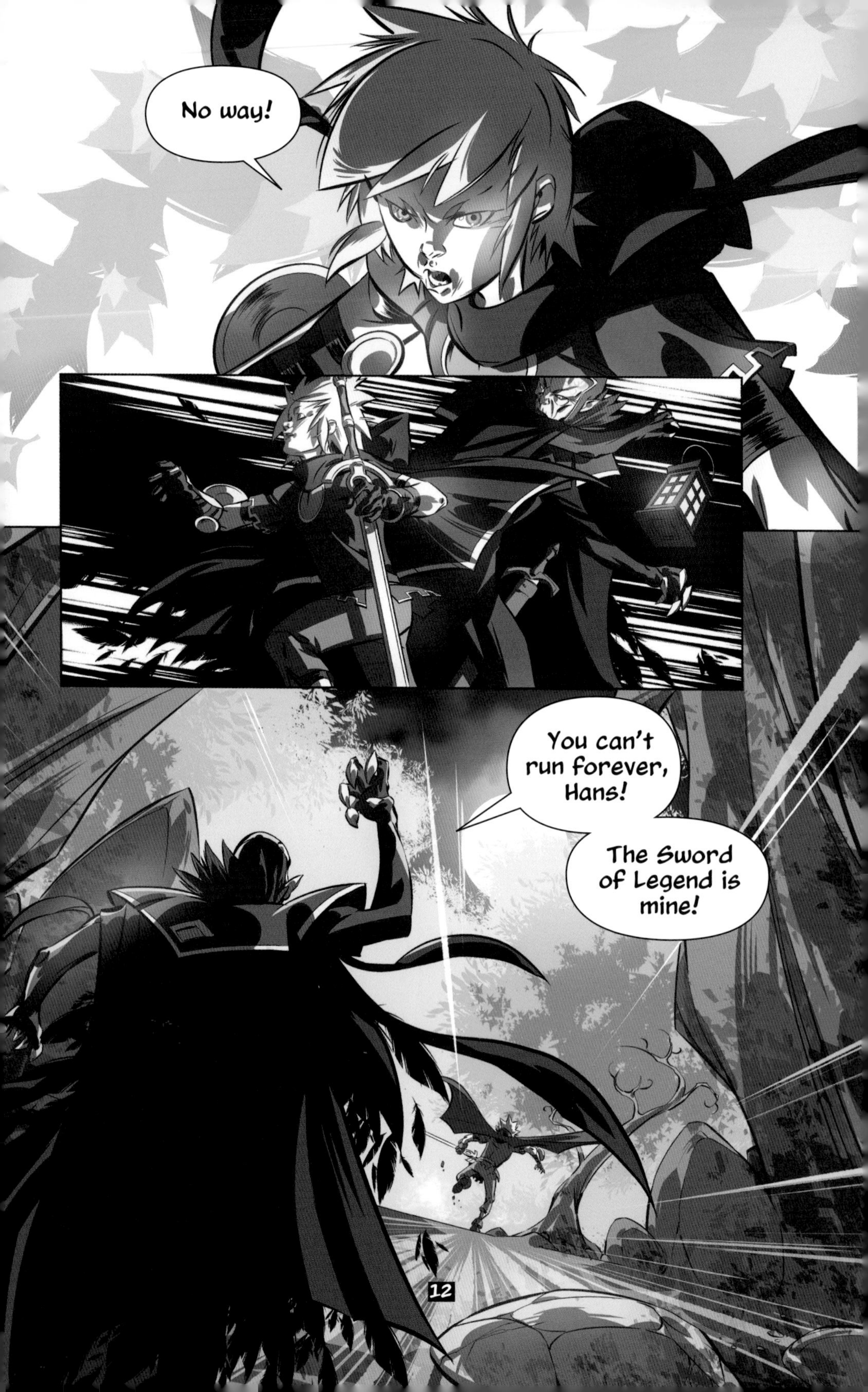
No way!
You can't run forever, Hans!
The Sword of Legend is mine!

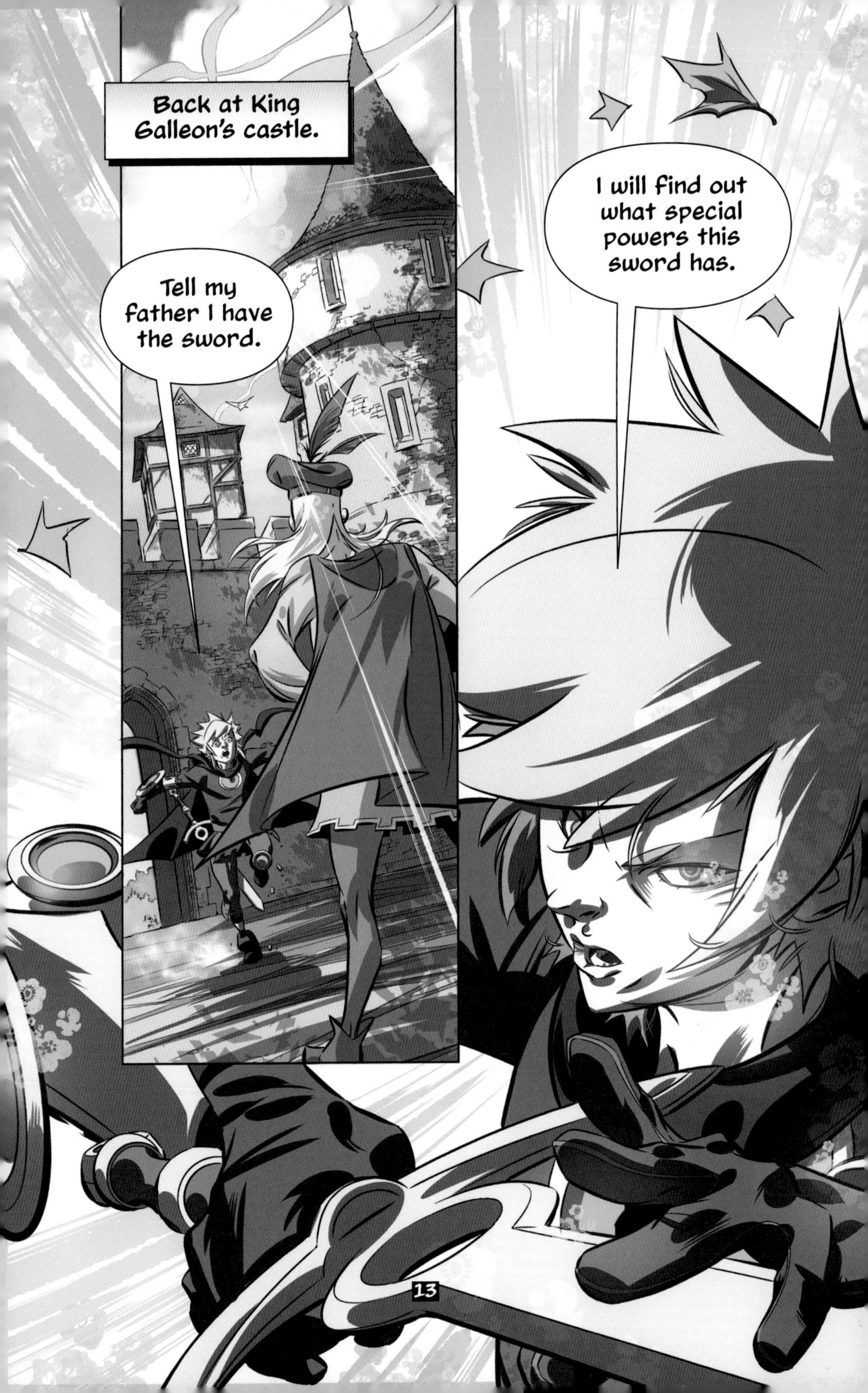
Back at King Galleon's castle.
Tell my father I have the sword.
I will find out what special powers this sword has.

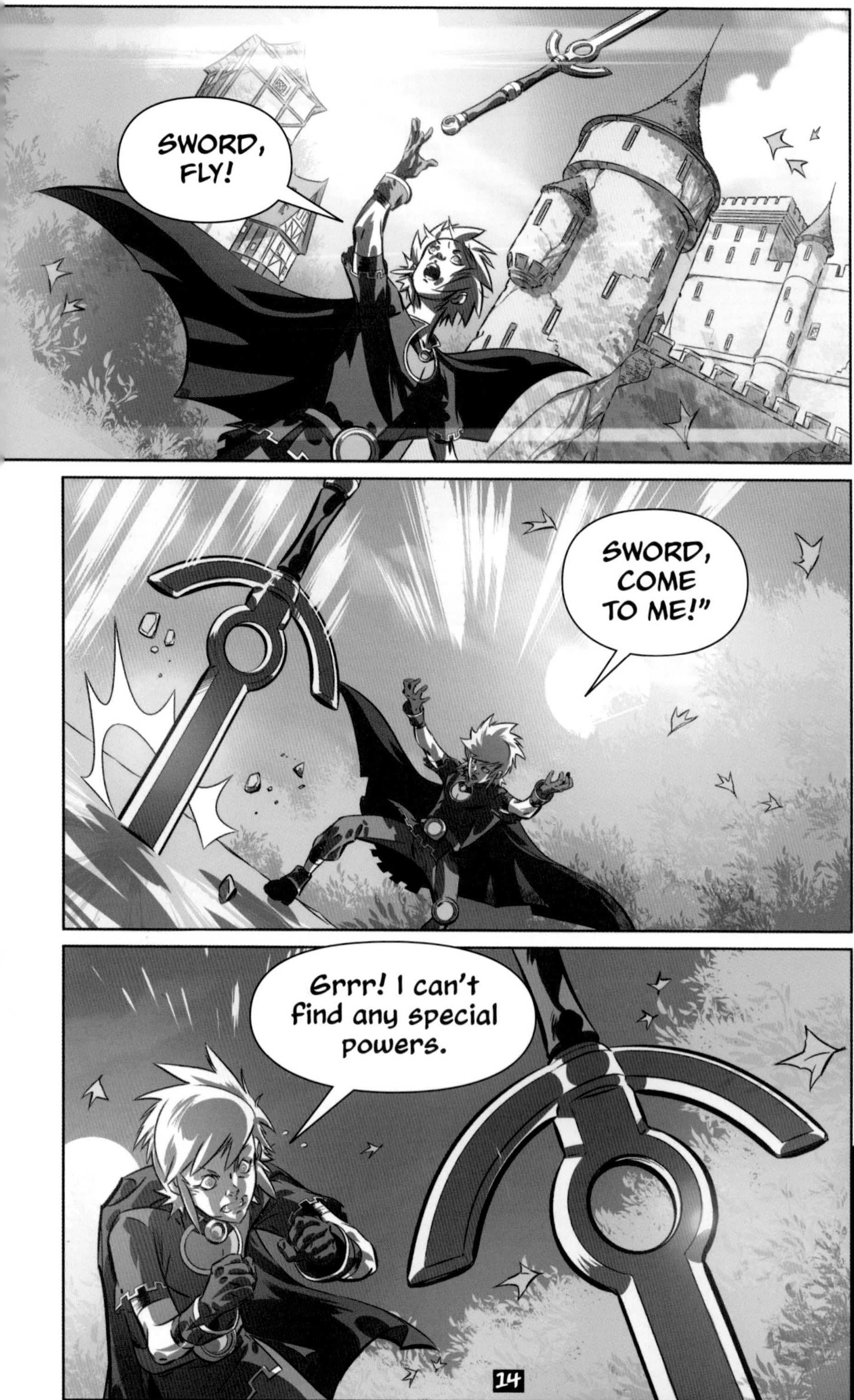
SWORD, FLY!
SWORD, COME TO ME!"
Grrr! I can't find any special powers.

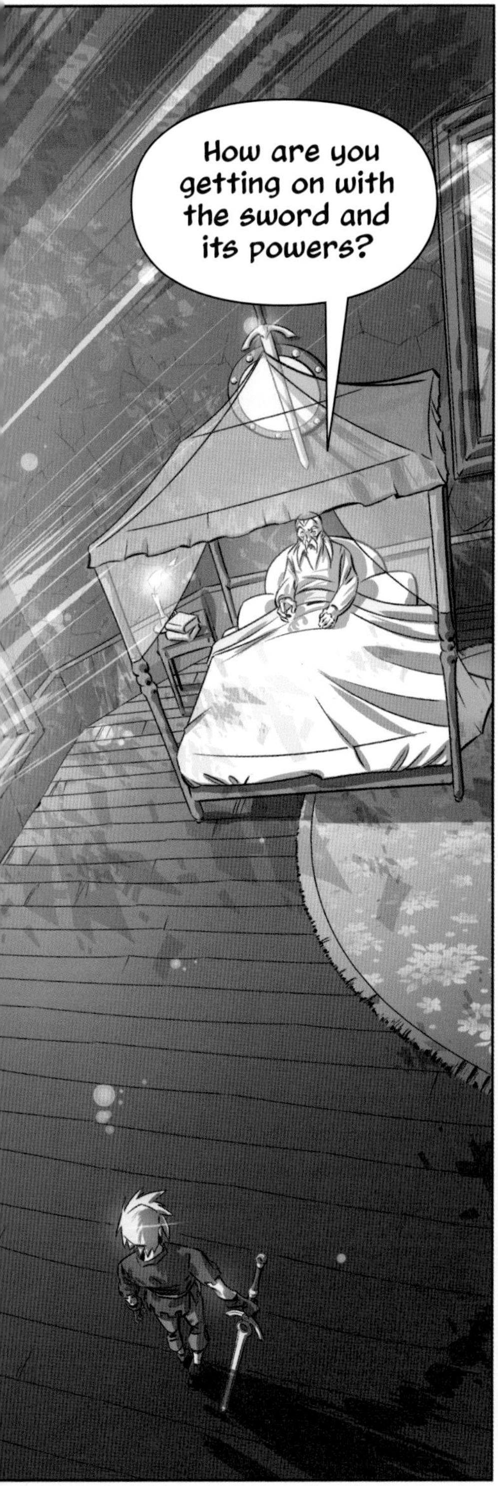
How are you getting on with the sword and its powers?

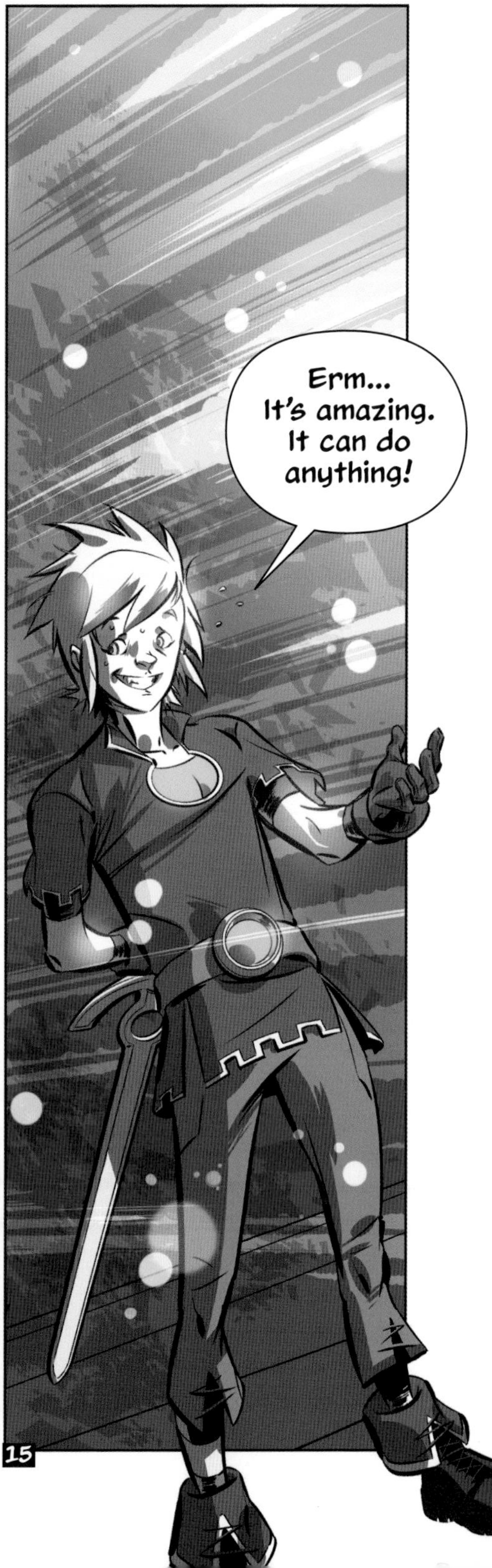
Erm... It's amazing. It can do anything!

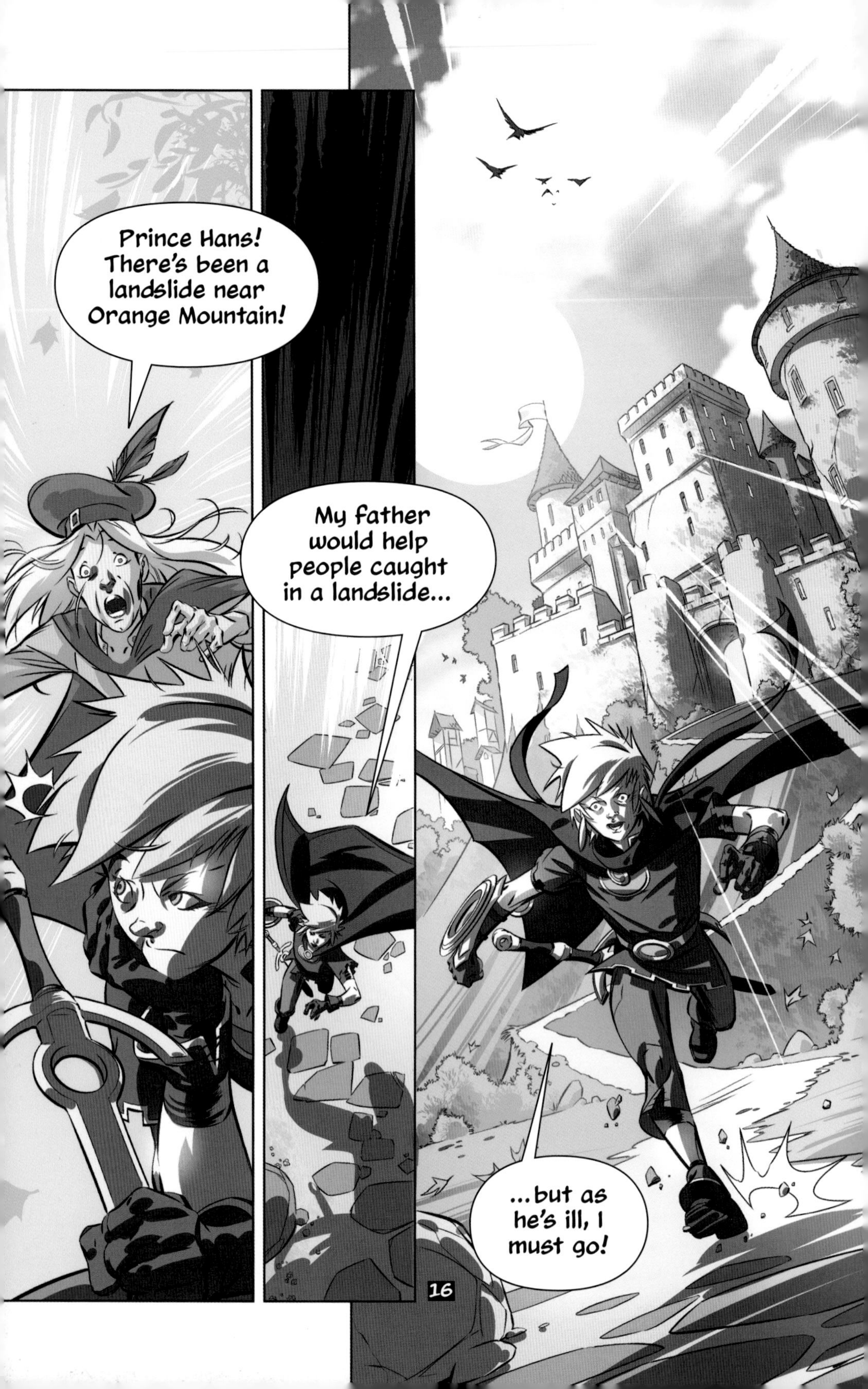
Prince Hans! There's been a landslide near Orange Mountain!
My father would help people caught in a landslide...
...but as he's ill, I must go!

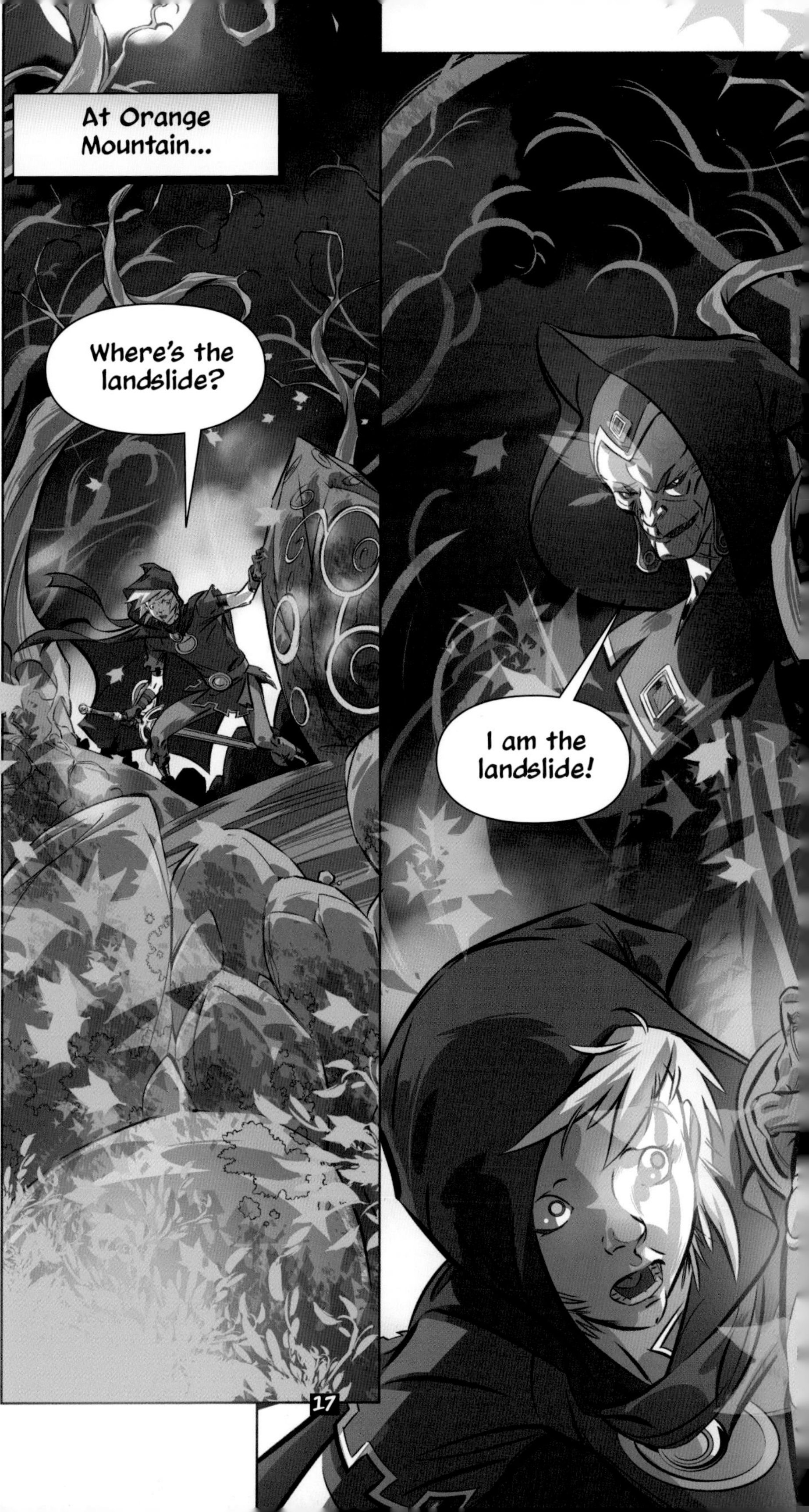
At Orange Mountain...
Where's the landslide?
I am the landslide!

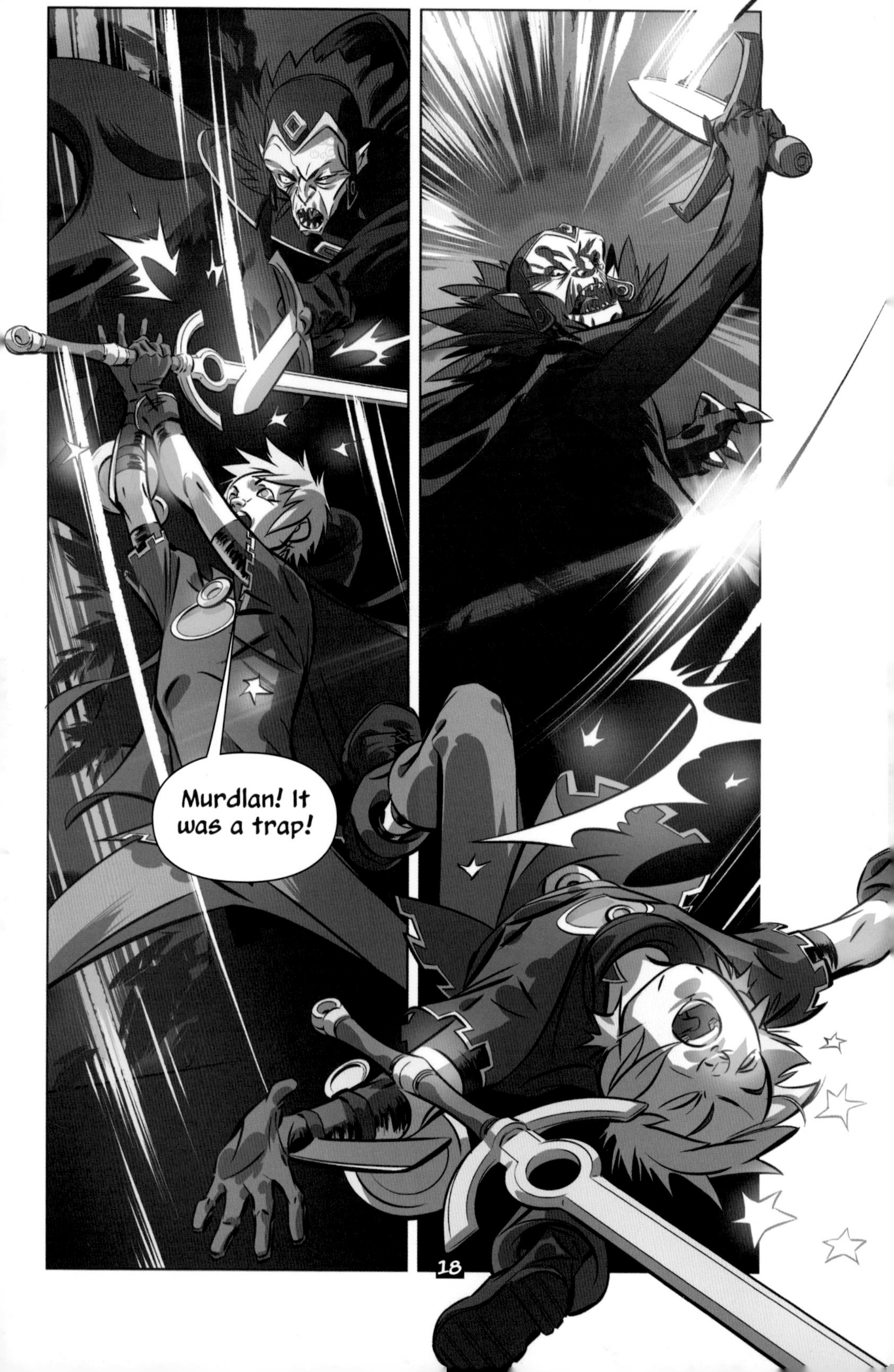
Murdlan! It was a trap!

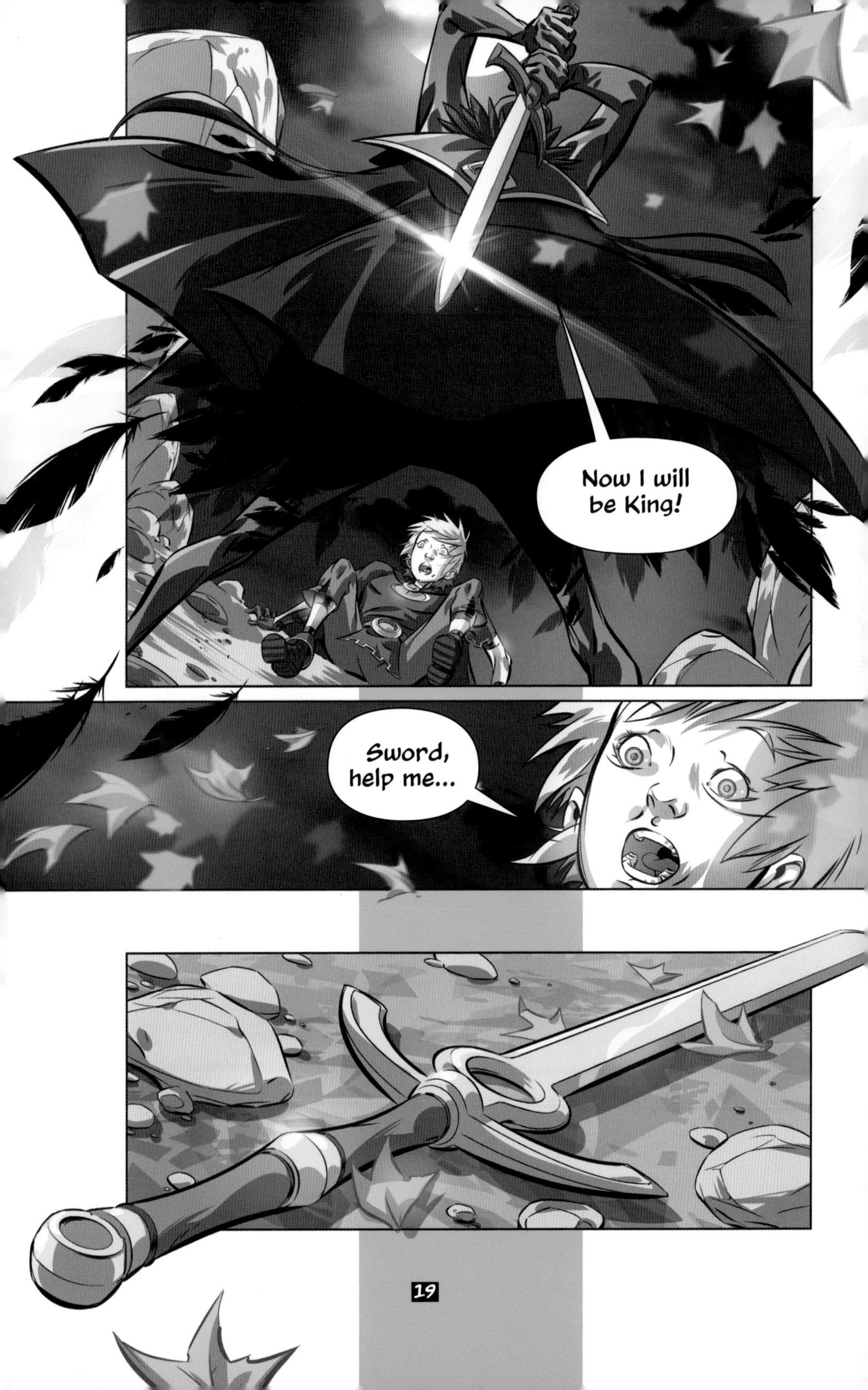
Now I will be King!
Sword, help me...

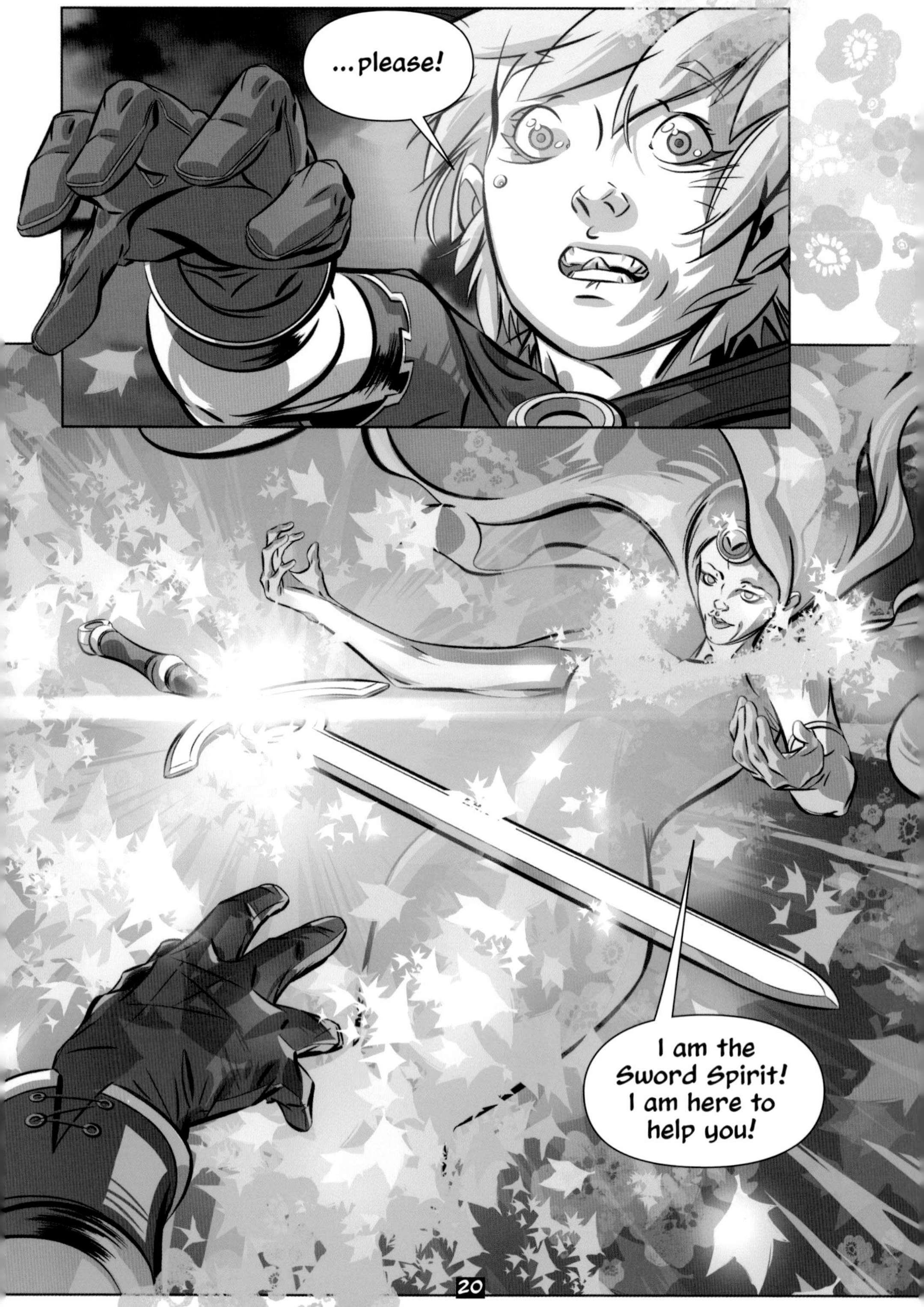
...please!
I am the Sword Spirit! I am here to help you!

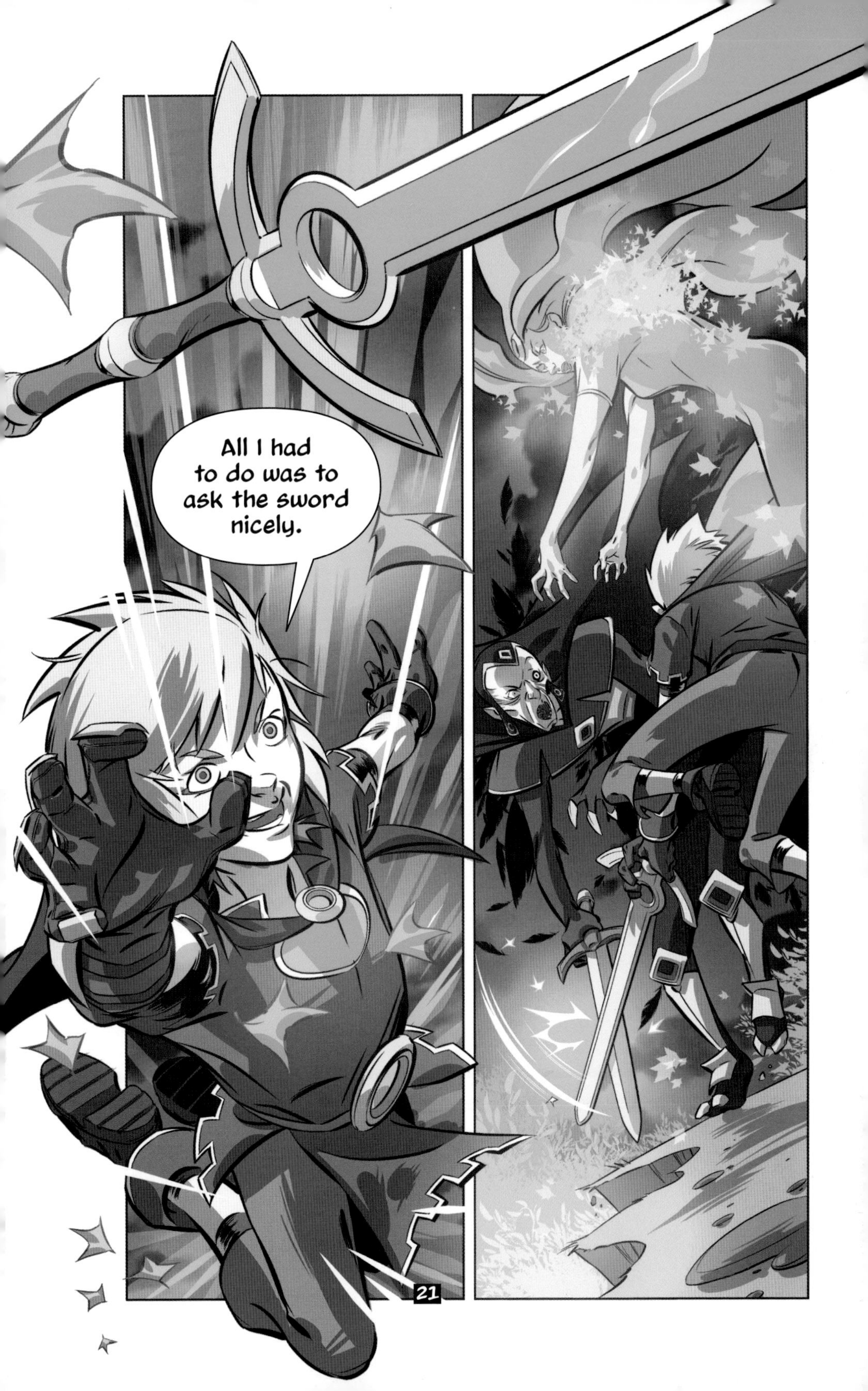
All I had to do was to ask the sword nicely.

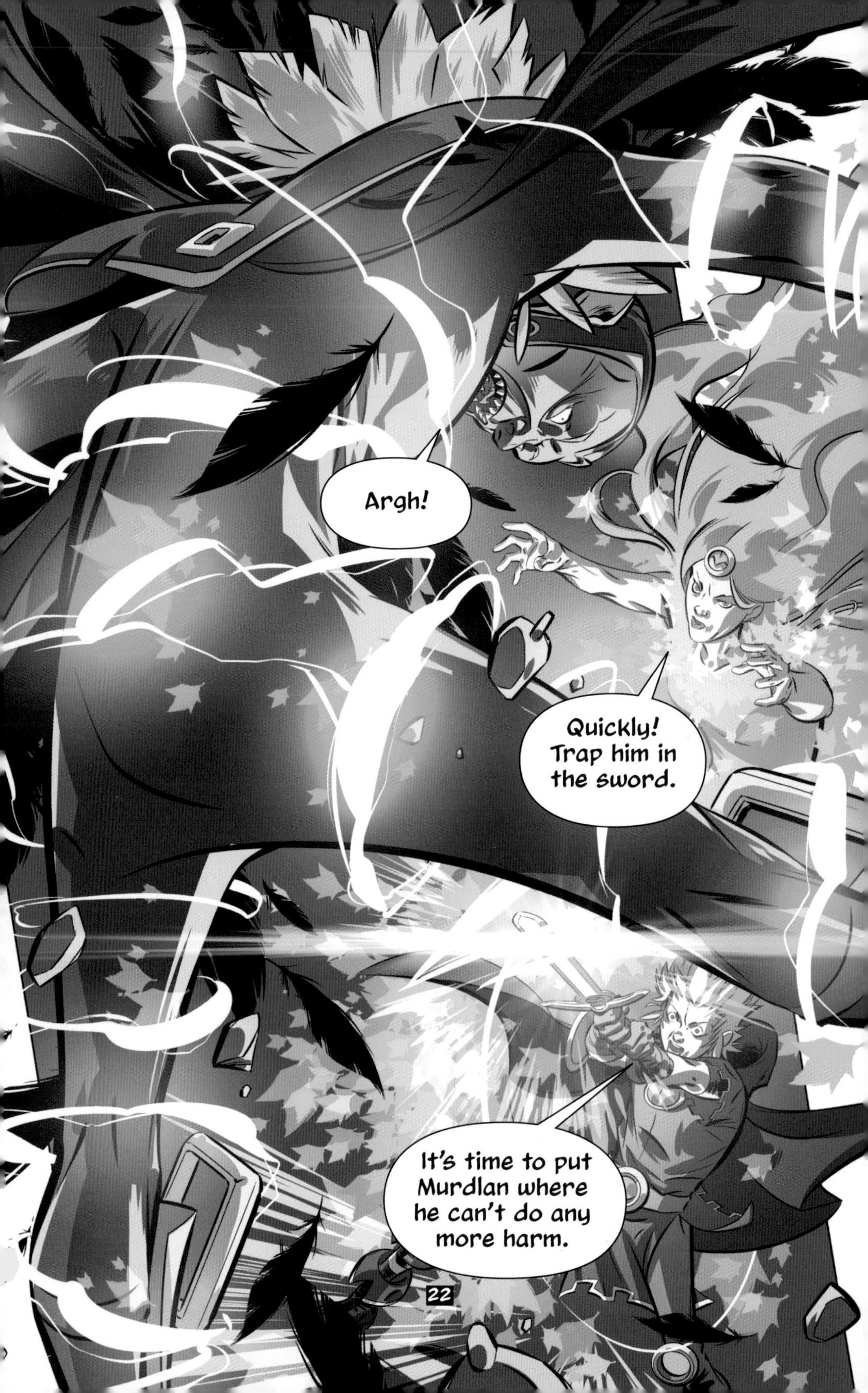
Argh!
Quickly! Trap him in the sword.
It's time to put Murdlan where he can't do any more harm.

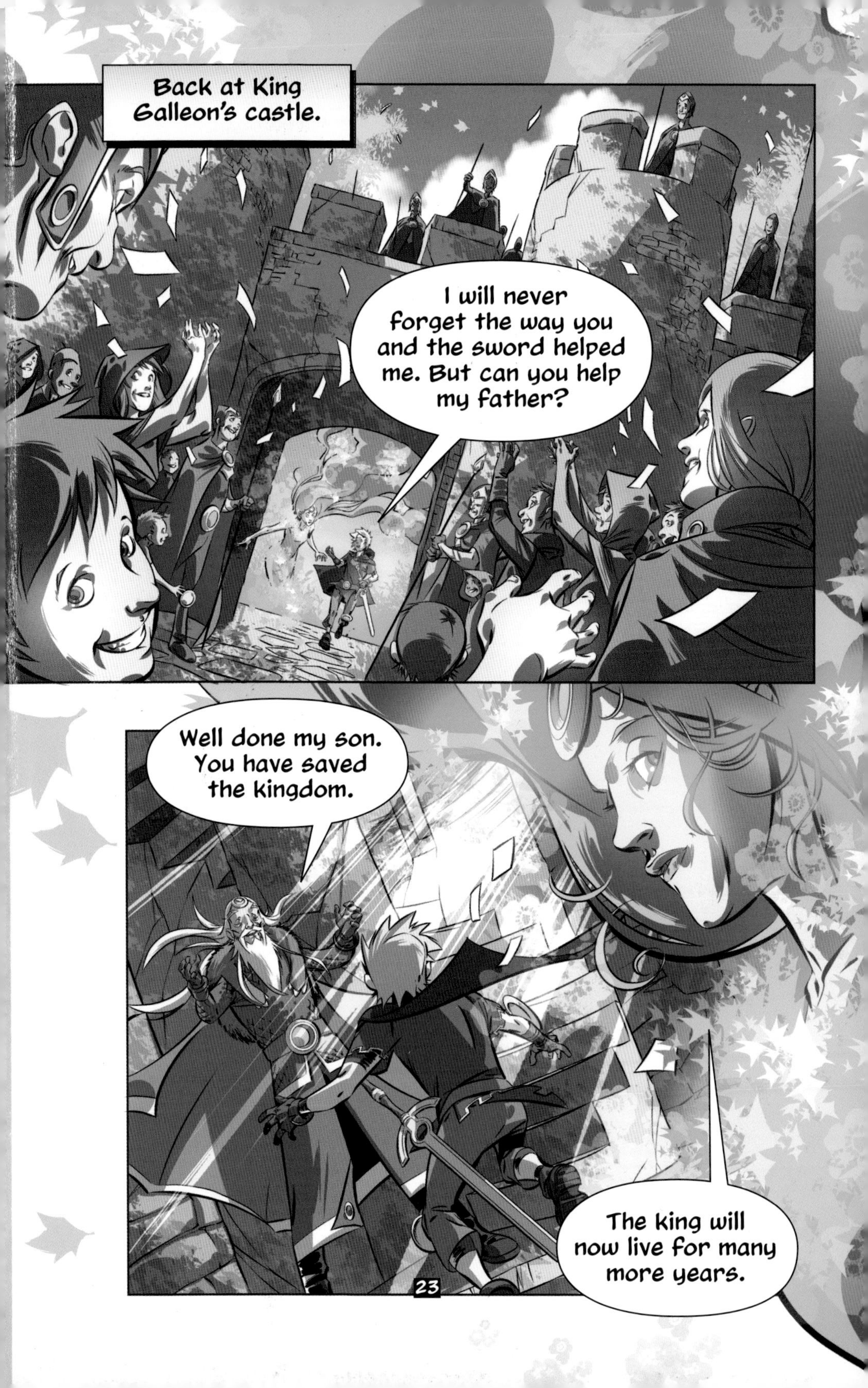
Back at King Galleon's castle.
I will never forget the way you and the sword helped me. But can you help my father?
Well done my son. You have saved the kingdom.
The king will now live for many more years.

About

SLIPSTREAM

Slipstream is a series of expertly levelled books designed for pupils who are struggling with reading. Its unique three-strand approach through fiction, graphic fiction and non-fiction gives pupils a rich reading experience that will accelerate their progress and close the reading gap.

At the heart of every Slipstream graphic fiction book is a great story. Easily accessible words and phrases ensure that pupils both decode and comprehend, and the high interest stories really engage older struggling readers.

Whether you're using Slipstream Level 1 for Guided Reading or as an independent read, here are some suggestions:

1. Make each reading session successful. Talk about the text or pictures before the pupil starts reading. Introduce any unfamiliar vocabulary.

2. Encourage the pupil to talk about the book using a range of open questions. For example, what would have happened if Hans had given Murdlan the Sword of Legend?

3. Discuss the differences between reading fiction, graphic fiction and non-fiction. What do they prefer?

Slipstream Level 1 photocopiable **WORKBOOK** ISBN: 978 1 4451 1798 0 available – download free sample worksheets from: www.franklinwatts.co.uk

For guidance, SLIPSTREAM Level 1 – Sword of Legend has been approximately measured to:

National Curriculum Level: 2c
Reading Age: 7.0–7.6
Book Band: Turquoise

ATOS: 1.7*
Guided Reading Level: H
Lexile® Measure (confirmed): 250L

*Please check actual Accelerated Reader™ book level and quiz availability at www.arbookfind.co.uk